BRAVE Santa

NANCY POYDAR

Holiday House / New York

Printed in the United States of America
www.holidayhouse.com
First Edition
1 3 5 7 9 10 8 6 4 2

LIBRARY OF CONGRESS CATALOGING-IN-PUBLICATION DATA

Poydar, Nancy
Brave Santa/Nancy Poydar. — 1st ed.
p. cm.
Summary: At Christmas time at the mall, Jack, who is very shy, finds that Santa Claus is shy too.

ISBN 0-8234-1821-9 (hardcover)
[1. Bashfulness — Fiction. 2. Santa Claus — Fiction. 3. Christmas — Fiction.]
I. Title.

PZ7.P8846Br 2004
[E]—dc22 2003056618

Designed by Yvette Lenhart

For Hank

Christmas
was around
the corner.

Jack could hardly wait to
decorate the tree.

He loved baking cookies.
He liked Santa too,
but he didn't want
to talk to him.

When the store clerk said,
"Merry Christmas, young man,"
Jack hid.

When the mailman said,
"I bet Santa's coming
to your house!"
Jack looked down
at his feet.

And when his mother asked,
"Do you want to sit
on Santa's lap?"
Jack shook his head,
No, no, no!

"You're shy, Jack,"
his father said. "It's
just a stage."

"Arrrrrrrr."

Jack whined like a siren through the house.

"What's that?" asked his mother.

"I'm practicing for when Santa brings me a fire engine."

"You're good at practicing," she said. "Practice talking to Santa so you can ask him for a fire engine."

"You be Santa," he said to Smudge. "I'll be Jack." Smudge dashed under the chair.

"You be Santa," he said to his father. "I'll be Jack."

"Ho, ho, ho, Jack! What do you want for Christmas?"

"A fire engine, please," said Jack.

"That's the spirit!" said Jack's father.

"Arrrrrrr." Jack whined up the stairs to bed.

The moon slipped behind a cloud.
"The moon is shy too," Jack told Smudge.
"It's just a stage."

One day they wrapped presents.
One night they decorated the tree.
Soon it was time for last-minute shopping.

At the mall a bear was giving out candy canes. Jack felt too shy to take one. The bow lady asked Jack to put his finger on the ribbon.

He still felt shy.
Santa's chair was empty.
"Maybe he went home," said Jack.

Then an elf was
coming toward Jack.
Jack slipped behind
a curtain.

WHUMP!

He bumped into
something big. It was
soft like a cloud,
but it was red . . .

...like Santa!

"Shhh, I'm hiding!" whispered Santa. "I'm not feeling very brave. I only talk to children once a year. All those boys and girls! Oh, dear!"

Now Jack had to speak up. "You're shy. I'm shy too. It's just a stage."

"But what can we do?" asked Santa.

"We can practice," said Jack. "I'm good at practicing! I'll be Jack and you be Santa."

Santa shook his head
up and down.

Then he said,
"Merry Christmas,
young man. What's your
name?"

"Jack."

"What would you like for
Christmas?" asked Santa.

"That's the spirit,"
said Jack.

"That's the spirit,"
said Santa.

They practiced until Santa
said, "I think I've got my
courage up now."

"Me too!" said Jack.

"We were afraid you were lost," said Jack's father.

"I was getting my courage up," said Jack. "To talk to Santa."

"Brave boy!" said Jack's father.

When his turn came, Jack whispered,
"How are you doing?"

"Watch this!" said Santa. "HO! HO! HO! Jack!
What do you want for Christmas?"

Jack spoke up. "A fire engine, please!"

"That's the spirit!" boomed Santa.

"BRAVE SANTA!" boomed Jack.

At last it was Christmas Eve. Jack tried to stay awake so he could talk with Santa again. But as the Christmas moon rose high in the sky . . .

Jack was dreaming his Christmas dream . . .

and Santa was too busy to talk.